Worms for Lunch?

LEONID GORE

Scholastic Press • New York

Who eats worms for lunch?

Not me!

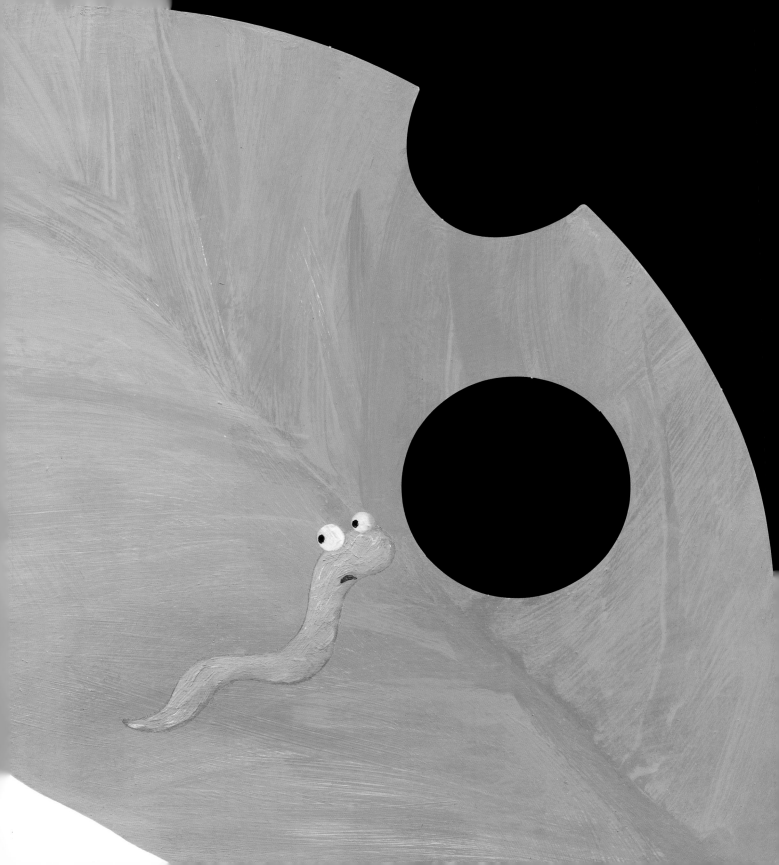

I like cheese!

Yummy!

I like a nice little mouse
for lunch. . . .

Or—a big bowl of milk . . .

Meow!

Milk is good.

But I like to munch
fresh green grass for lunch.

Doesn't everyone?

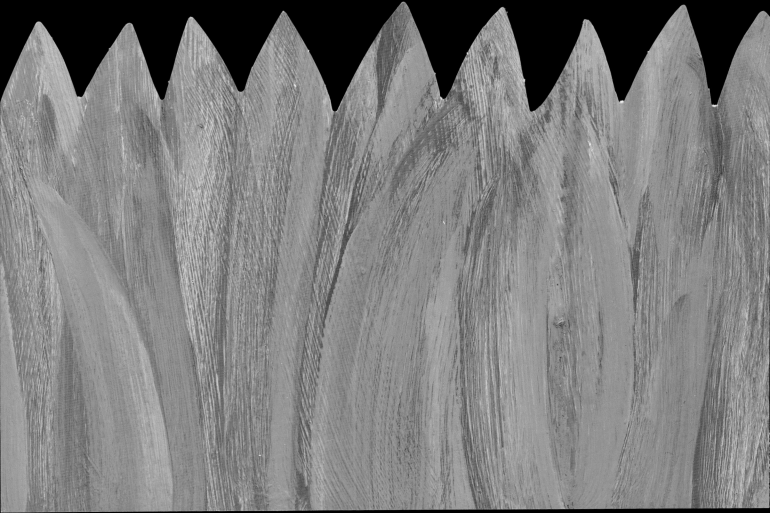

Grass?

Not me!!!

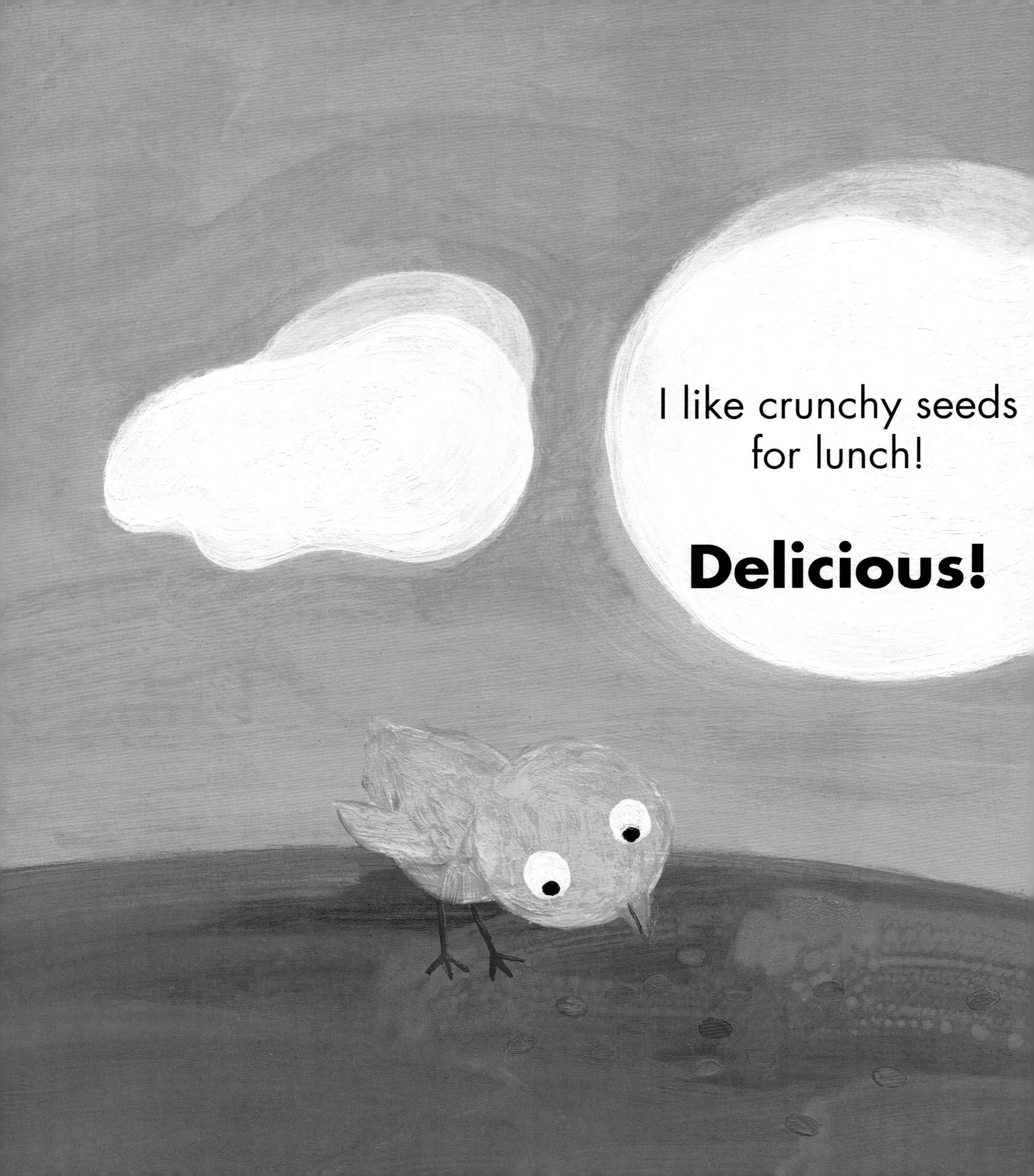

I like crunchy seeds for lunch!

Delicious!

Seeds are much too dry for me.
I love to sip the sweet,
sweet nectar of a flower.

Buzz-z-z-z

And I
love
ice cream
even more!

Ice cream for lunch?

Not for me . . .

I prefer fresh fish,
of course!

Slurp!

And what do fish like?

Fish love wiggly, wiggly worms for lunch!
YUM, YUM!

You can't eat me. . . .
I'm a character in
this book!

Bye!

To Andrew Zimmern,
who *has* tried worms for lunch!
—L.G.

Library of Congress Cataloging-in-Publication Data

Gore, Leonid.
Worms for lunch? / Leonid Gore. — 1st ed.   p. cm.
Summary: Easy-to-read text and die-cut illustrations allow
various creatures to reveal what they like to eat.
ISBN 978-0-545-24338-4 (hardcover)
1. Toy and movable books—Specimens. [1. Animals—Food—Fiction.
2. Food habits—Fiction. 3. Toy and movable books.] I. Title.
PZ7.G659993Wp 2011   [E]—dc22   2010004023
10 9 8 7 6 5 4 3 2 1   11 12 13 14 15

Printed in Malaysia   108
First edition, March 2011

The display type was set in ITC Garamond Ultra.
The text was set in Futura Book and Futura Bold.
The art was created using acrylic on paper.
Book design by Marijka Kostiw

I like worms, too!